TIME RANGERS

2. A Blast From the Past

"C'mon, Rangers!" urged their captain. "Let's show 'em we mean business."

Jacko led by example as usual. His sleeves rolled up, he crunched into his next tackle in midfield, winning the ball cleanly and playing it forward to Ryan. "Go for goal!" he yelled.

Rangers' leading scorer never needed any such encouragement. By instinct, he turned with the ball to create a shooting angle for himself outside the Braves' penalty area but was crudely upended by his marker.

Ryan jumped to his feet and glared at the big defender. "Dirty foul, that. Back off, will you, and keep the plague to yourself!"

TIME RANGERS

2. A Blast From the Past

Rob Childs

Hippo

DAZZA
GOAL KEEPER — 1

WORM
RIGHT-BACK — 2

STOPPER
CENTRE-BACK — 5

RAKESH
RIGHT-MIDFIELD — 4

MR STOPPARD
MANAGER

791,894
£2·99

JACKO
CENTRE-MIDFIELD — 8

SPEEDIE
RIGHT-WINGER — 7

RYAN
CENTRE-FORWARD — 9

ANIL
LEFT-WINGER — 11

MR THOMAS
MANAGER

For my wife Joy, with special thanks

Scholastic Children's Books,
Commonwealth House, 1–19 New Oxford Street,
London WC1A 1NU, UK
a division of Scholastic Ltd
London ~ New York ~ Toronto ~ Sydney ~ Auckland

First published in the UK by Scholastic Ltd, 1997

ISBN 0 439 01125 6

Typeset by DP Photosetting, Aylesbury, Bucks.
Printed by Cox & Wyman Ltd, Reading, Berks.

3 5 7 9 10 8 6 4

1 Strike camp

"Tick!" cried Dazza, nipping round the tent. "You've got the plague!"

"No, I haven't, you missed me," claimed Rakesh.

"Rubbish! Got you on the back."

Mr Thomas broke off from supervising other lads trying to dismantle their tents. "Hey! Stop messing about," he bellowed. "We want to strike camp in twenty minutes."

The co-manager of Tanfield Rangers Under-12s was anxious not to arrive late for the second match of their Easter soccer tour – against the Barwell Braves.

They were faced with quite a drive up to higher ground in the Peak District and he wasn't sure how long it would take in the hired minibuses.

His son Ryan weaved by, dribbling a football between the tents and ticked Rakesh as he went past. "Struck by plague, Rakky, pass it on."

Dazza laughed. "Now you've got double-plague!"

"Huh! About the only thing Ryan's passed to me all season. He sure never passes the ball."

"Doesn't need to. His job is to score goals," said Dazza. "How many did you get this season? One, was it? And even that was an own goal!"

"OK, OK, but what a beauty!" grinned Rakesh. "Perfect lob, right in the top corner. Beat you all ends up. Ryan would have been proud of it."

"Will you two get a move on?" demanded Mr Thomas, striding towards them. "We'll be playing Barwell under floodlights at this rate."

"Is it true that all the people of Barwell died of the plague?" the Rangers' goalkeeper asked him.

"No, but I think most of the village was wiped out by it," the manager replied. "So no tasteless plague jokes when we get there, understand?"

"As if we would," said Dazza innocently.

"I'm just warning you, that's all," Mr Thomas said. "If it hadn't been for the villagers' bravery, the plague might have spread far and wide."

"What did they do?" put in Rakesh.

Mr Thomas hesitated, uncertain of the full facts of the story. "Look, I haven't got time to give you a history lesson right now. If you really want to know more about it, you know who to ask."

"Worm!" they chorused.

"Right!" the manager grinned, bending

to start pulling out the guy ropes. "That boy seems to be a walking encyclopaedia about history."

"Yeah, and just as boring," Dazza cackled. "Give me CD-ROM any time!"

A football suddenly whizzed over their heads, just missing Mr Thomas. "Hey! Who kicked that?" he yelled.

"Soz, Dad," Ryan giggled. "Just practising my volleys."

Mr Thomas was not amused. "Well make sure any you do in the match aren't so wild. Now get cracking on that tent of yours."

After their match on Easter Sunday the footballers had camped for two nights in a field next to Oakbrooke monastery. For six of the players, the ruins conjured up memories of the amazing adventure that had begun there.

"I'll never forget that place," murmured Jacko, the team captain, as he stared at it for the last time. "Still can't

believe what happened to us."

"Neither can I," sighed Stopper. "Seems like another world."

"It was. Over six hundred years ago."

"C'mon, Keith, quit rabbiting," said Mr Stoppard, his dad and Rangers' joint manager. "Got to get a move on. All aboard!"

The two men counted the lads as they climbed into the minibuses and fastened their seat belts. "One short. Who's that?" asked Mr Thomas.

"Worm, as usual," laughed Ryan. "And we all know where he'll be!"

"Typical! Might have known it," muttered Mr Thomas. "You lot stay here and I'll go and fetch him."

He found Michael Winter, as expected, in the monastery ruins. Worm was sitting on the stump of a stone pillar, gazing through the one remaining small archway towards the market town of Oakbrooke. The boy hadn't responded to any of his calls, so lost was he in his own dream world.

"There you are, Worm, er, Michael," he said. "You were beginning to get me worried, disappearing like that again."

"I haven't disappeared," answered Worm wistfully. "I've been here all the time. There's no going back – I've tried."

"We're not going back anywhere," said Mr Thomas, puzzled. "We're going on – on to Barwell. You'll like it there. The place is full of history."

Worm nodded slowly. "Yeah, but it's not like actually being there at the time, you know, when things really happened."

"Who'd want to be there during the plague?" he snorted. "Anyway, you can't go back in time, can you? No such thing as time travel."

Worm stood up and looked around at the ruined site. "No, I thought so as well," he said under his breath. "Until this week!"

"What a stupid goal to go and give away!"

None of the Rangers' defence wanted to look the captain in the eye.

"Sorry, Jacko," Stopper mumbled, staring down at some imaginary hole in his boot. "Should have cut that pass out."

"Not just your fault," Jacko stormed on. "The marking was nowhere. That kid could have had his dinner before he scored!"

The other defenders all pretended to be busy doing something, hoping to escape any personal blame. Only Dazza was doing an actual job, the one he hated most – picking the ball out of the back of the net.

The goalie hoofed it angrily upfield so that the game could restart. He was mad at himself for letting the ball slip under his body as he dived on it, but took his temper out on his defence. "No good moaning at them, Jacko. They think marking is what teachers do in their books."

The two team managers were equally critical of the way the Rangers had started the game. "Still half asleep, some of 'em!" griped Mr Thomas on the touchline. "I could tell they weren't in the right frame of mind for a match when we were back in the camp."

"All too much of a rush, getting here," observed Mr Stoppard. "We didn't have a chance to get them warmed up properly. Got caught cold."

"Hardly surprising," added Mr Thomas with a shiver, tugging his coat's zip right up to his collar. "It's freezing up here!"

"We're in the High Peak now. Not so sheltered as down in the dales. The wind's coming at us across the moors. Even looks like it might snow!"

"Come on, mark up!" Mr Thomas yelled out at the players in frustration. "Get those tackles in. They're all over us."

Rakesh was among the group of substitutes nearby. "Nobody wants to get too close," he hissed. "Bet they're worried about catching the plague."

Mr Stoppard overheard his comment. "Catching the plague!" he snorted. "That was centuries ago. I've heard you people come out with some excuses this season, but that just about beats the lot!"

2 Pass it on!

"C'mon, Rangers!" urged their captain. "Let's show 'em we mean business."

Jacko led by example as usual. His sleeves rolled up, he crunched into his next tackle in midfield, winning the ball cleanly and playing it forward to Ryan. "Go for goal!" he yelled.

Rangers' leading scorer never needed any such encouragement. By instinct, he turned with the ball to create a shooting angle for himself outside the Braves' penalty area but was crudely upended by his marker.

Ryan jumped to his feet and glared at

the big defender. "Dirty foul, that. Back off, will you, and keep the plague to yourself!"

"No need for that kind of talk, lad," said the referee to calm him down. "You've got a free-kick."

"Only joking, ref," Ryan said, slipping the official a sly grin. He knew that Dad wouldn't tolerate any dissent on the field.

Ryan and Jacko waited while the home side organized a defensive wall of bodies to try and block the free-kick. "You or me?" the striker asked.

"You," said Jacko. "I'll make it look as if I'm going to whack it and you follow up behind me."

That suited Ryan fine. He always fancied his chances from this range. As Jacko ran over the ball, Ryan loped in and deliberately curled the ball around the wall. The Barwell Braves' goalkeeper, Daniel, never even moved, but at the last second the ball veered away from the target, clipping the outside of the upright.

"Unlucky!" Jacko cried. "Great effort. Next one will go in."

It didn't, sadly, but at least the match became a far more even contest than before, with both teams doing their fair share of the attacking.

Dazza excelled himself with one full-length, fingertip save, but he needed a spot of extra help to deal with another. Although he managed to take the sting off the shot, the ball would still have crept into the goal if Worm hadn't scurried back to sweep it off the line.

"Thanks, Worm, good covering there," Dazza grinned sheepishly. "Just testing to see if you can run as fast as you read."

Worm smiled back, pleased to receive some praise for a change from his critical keeper. And it was Rangers' bookish full-back who also started the move up the right wing that resulted in their well-deserved equalizer.

Worm linked up with Jacko in his own half and then looped the ball over Speedie's head for the winger to chase. Speedie lived up to his name, leaving his marker for dead as he cut inside with the ball. His cross-shot beat Daniel's dive and was on its way into the goal until Ryan arrived in time to blast the ball into the bulging net.

"Just making sure," he said, winking at Speedie. "Shoot first, ask questions later, that's my motto."

"I've noticed," Speedie grunted. "That's three goals of mine you've pinched this season."

Jacko ran up to congratulate them both. "Doesn't matter who scores them as long as they go in," he said, knowing Ryan didn't believe that for a minute.

Ryan was a born goalscorer, selfish and single-minded, determined that if anybody was to have the final touch, it was going to be his boot that sent the ball over the goal-line.

"You're beginning to play some decent football at last," Mr Stoppard told them at the break. "Keep passing that ball about and make spaces."

"We've got their attackers under control now," Stopper said confidently to his dad. "They won't score again."

"Nor will we unless we have a few more shots at goal ourselves," put in Mr Thomas quickly, still not satisfied with the team's performance. "It's about time a few more of you got your names on the score-sheet."

"They'll have to get to the ball before I do, then," Ryan boasted.

"Oh, they will," his dad said with a smirk. "Because you won't be there. You're coming off soon."

791,896

"Not again! I was subbed last game as well."

"Right, so you'll be used to it, won't you? Go on, you've still got about ten minutes to bag another goal."

Rakesh went on at the start of the second half as snowflakes began to swirl down from a threatening sky. "Must be part of the tactics, wearing our change strip of all-white today," he joked. "If the snow gets heavier, Barwell won't be able to see us in this camouflage kit."

As Tanfield Rangers kicked off, Jacko clapped his hands for attention. "Treat the ball as if it's got the plague," he cried. "Pass it on!"

Ryan had no intention of passing the ball to anyone. As left-winger Anil tapped it to him, the striker lashed the ball goalwards right from the centre-circle. It caught Daniel unawares, gazing up at the snowflakes, and only the desperate cries of his teammates made him realize the danger.

The keeper panicked when he saw the ball whirling towards him. Daniel slipped and fell over, lying helpless on the ground while the ball bounced by out of his reach. Then he breathed a huge sigh of relief as he watched it bobble past the post out of play.

Daniel's good fortune did not last. Two minutes later he was beaten again by Ryan, and this time the net saved him another journey to fetch the ball. Receiving a quick pass from Anil, Ryan burst through a gap and took the shortest route to goal.

He was confident enough in his shooting not to bother trying to dribble round the advancing keeper. Ryan simply glanced up to set his sights and then let fly. His arm was up in the air to celebrate his success even before the net was called into action.

The Braves fought back briefly, striving to get back on level terms, but a third goal killed them off. Speedie made the most of Ryan's early exit, switching to play more in the middle, and he was in the right place to meet Anil's accurate cross on the half-volley and steer the ball home.

There was no further scoring, however, until just before the end of the game. As the snow flurries increased, covering the pitch with a thin white coat, the game's crowning glory was bestowed on a most unlikely head – that of Rakesh.

The midfielder found himself in the Braves' penalty area just as Jacko's cross whistled over straight at him. He had no option but to head it, and the ball deflected beyond the keeper's straining fingertips into the far corner of the goal to cap a fine 4-1 win for the tourists.

Rakesh's joy knew no bounds. He ran around in circles like a clockwork toy that had gone out of control until finally pinned down to the snowy ground by his amazed teammates.

Rakesh didn't mind all their jokes after the match. He sat on a bench in the cloakroom of the village hall with a big silly grin on his face, reliving the great moment.

"Don't even care if I do go and catch the plague now," he mused happily. "At least I've got a goal as well!"

3 Church guide

The players had lunch in Barwell village hall, sitting together at small groups of tables to enjoy a much needed hot meal. Worm and Rakesh found themselves alongside Daniel Buxton, the home team's goalie.

"Rakky here would like your autograph as a souvenir," Worm said, straight-faced. "For letting him score his first goal."

"Ignore him," Rakesh grinned. "I score loads of goals."

"In your dreams, maybe," smiled Worm.

"Reckon I'll have nightmares about

your centre-forward," Daniel replied. "I was sure glad to see the back of him when he went off."

"You're lucky," said Worm. "We've got to put up with Ryan all week."

"Sorry for any stupid jokes about the plague," Rakesh said sheepishly.

"It's OK, we're used to it," Daniel shrugged. "My family have always lived in Barwell, you know, going way back before plague times."

Worm immediately perked up. "Did any of them die of the plague?"

"Ten, as far as I know. Nearly the end of us Buxtons, that was. Only three of the family survived."

The conversations on the table around them were all about the match, but Worm kept pestering the goalie for more information on how the villagers coped when the plague struck.

"You a history freak or something?" asked Daniel.

"Worm's just a freak!" quipped Rakesh.

Daniel smiled. "I'll show you around after the meal, if you like," he offered. "There's a few things to see that might interest you."

"You bet they will!" Worm beamed.

"Take a look at these," said Daniel, inviting Worm to examine some scratch marks on the stonework in the south aisle of Barwell church. "What do you make of them?"

Worm peered more closely and ran his fingertips over the well-worn grooves. "If I didn't know any better, I'd say somebody has tried to carve some stick figures playing football."

"That's exactly what they're doing! My great, great, umpteen great grandad, Will Buxton, did them during the plague when he was just a kid."

"Probably the earliest example of

soccer graffiti!" Worm laughed. "Bet he got a good hiding for damaging the church wall."

Daniel shrugged in response. "Maybe, but the family spent a lot of time in here that year and I suppose Will was bored."

Worm nodded and gazed around the small church. He would have liked to explore it properly, but he guessed someone would come to fetch him soon. His attention switched back to the scratches.

"One of the figures seems to have just kicked the ball and another's jumping up to head it," he said, touching the outlines of the shapes.

"Dead right! Football's been played here in the village ever since the Civil War. They say it even helped the people to last out the plague."

"How on earth did it do that?"

"It's a long story. You know how the village cut itself off from the outside world when the plague broke out?" Daniel began. "Well, apparently, the whole thing nearly went wrong. The tale goes that some of the younger folk were planning to run away one night and escape..."

"Deserters!" Worm cut in. "They'd have spread the plague elsewhere!"

"Probably. Fortunately, they got hold of a ball somehow, and playing football gave them something to do. Kept their spirits up, like."

"Wonder where the ball came from?" Worm mused for a moment. "Anyway, it was really tremendous the way the villagers were willing to risk death themselves to try and save others."

"That's why our team is called the Barwell Braves," Daniel replied proudly and pointed up to the window above their heads. "See that?"

"Wow! A stained-glass window dedicated to football!" gasped Worm. He

stared up in amazement as the daylight streaming through the window picked out all the colourful details of an ancient game of football on the village green. The scene was remarkably vivid and Worm felt the small hairs prickle on the back of his neck.

"That big stone cross isn't meant to be a goalpost, is it?" he asked.

"No, it's a wayside cross that still stands on the old packhorse trail nearby," Daniel explained. "It's where the people used to pick up all their vital supplies while they couldn't stray far from the village."

"It's a fantastic window!" Worm enthused. "Who had it made?"

"Will Buxton, of course!" grinned Daniel. "When Will grew up, he actually became the rector of this church and he wanted a special memorial to all the people who sacrificed their lives."

"Incredible how things work out

sometimes, isn't it?" Worm murmured.

Ryan burst noisily into the church at that point to collect him. "C'mon!" he cried. "Dad's revving up the engine like a rally driver. He wants to get to the new campsite before the snow gets any worse."

"Sorry, Daniel," Worm apologized. "Got to go. Pity! I'd love to have seen that wayside cross."

"Another time, maybe," the boy said, giving one of his little shrugs.

Worm took a last, lingering look at the beautiful stained-glass window. "Yeah, another time..." he sighed.

4 Roundheads!

As the minibuses turned into the moor-land campsite, the snow flurries began to increase in strength. "Drat this weather!" cursed Mr Thomas. "Didn't expect to have any snow this week. It's supposed to be springtime now."

"We've brought winter with us," Rakesh cackled. "Michael Winter!"

"Thought it might be my fault," Worm grumbled.

"Well, you do keep holding us up," Jacko said. "Whenever we want to set off somewhere, you've gone missing."

"Can't help being interested in

learning about things, can I?"

"Can't help being nosy, you mean," Ryan jibed. "Look where it's led us already this week!"

"Where's that?" Mr Thomas interrupted, stopping by the site office.

"Oh, doesn't matter, Dad. Just teasing old Worm about his history."

"He'll feel quite at home here, anyway. I've read that there's a small stone circle near this site and some prehistoric burial mounds."

Worm was out of the steamed-up bus almost before the driver, but he was in for a disappointment. Visibility was still restricted, this time by the snowflakes swirling about in the cold wind. "Right, first chance I get, I'm off for a closer look at that circle," he promised himself.

The attention of the rest, however, was caught by a towering outcrop of gritstone rock that loomed up over the campsite. "Wicked!" exclaimed Ryan.

"C'mon, gang. Last one up to the top shares a tent with Worm tonight!"

They all laughed, but were halted in their tracks by the booming voice of Mr Stoppard. "Not so fast, you guys! Nobody goes anywhere until we get the tents up. If we let you lot loose on those rocks, we'd never see you again till your stomachs told you it was teatime."

"This may be a shot in the dark," said Mr Thomas, re-emerging from the office, "but let me guess whose idea it was to go rock climbing…"

"Ryan!" came the chorus, saving him the bother of naming his own son.

"Trying to skive out of doing jobs as usual, eh?" he grinned. "Work comes before play, I'm afraid. Let's go and decide where to pitch camp."

Despite the discomfort of the bad weather, the boys erected their tents again in record time, fortified by a hot drink brewed by Stopper and Anil.

"Can't wait to get right up on top of those rocks," said Jacko, putting down his cup. "Should be able to see for miles."

"Not today, you won't," muttered Worm.

"Don't go wandering off," Mr Stoppard warned them all, "and keep an eye on the weather. You have to treat it with respect in the Peak District. Even though the snow's eased now, it can change again very quickly."

"Better to go and explore the stone circle instead," Worm suggested.

"You're obsessed with loads of old stones," snorted Ryan.

"Just what do you think those rocks of yours are, then?" Worm sneered back, but it was no use. They dragged him up on to his feet and hauled him away towards the spectacular outcrop that attracted them like a magnet.

They were soon glad to have Worm

with them. Something very strange was about to happen that nobody else could have understood...

"Gotcha!" yelled Ryan, slapping Worm hard on the back and then scampering away up a rough path through the boulders that littered the steep gritstone crag. "You've got the plague now."

"You're supposed to tick people, not thump them," Worm complained. "Anyway, I'm not playing that stupid game."

"Why not?" challenged Ryan, staying warily out of range. He still had a football tucked snugly under his arm, ever hopeful of the chance for a kickabout, even up high on the rocks.

"'Cos I don't think it's right. Not after we've been to Barwell."

"That's history! We're just having a bit of fun."

Worm plonked himself on a flat slab

of rock in defiance, staring out over the white landscape below. The seven mis-shapen stones of the ancient circle reared up in the distance like black, broken teeth.

He pulled up his fur hood to shut out the biting blasts of wind and also Ryan's taunts. The next thing Worm knew he was surrounded, with Jacko standing squarely in front of him. "We agree with you, Worm."

"What?" He tugged down his hood, thinking he must have misheard.

"You're right," Rakesh nodded. "It's about time we dropped all this plague business."

"We want to play something else instead," put in Anil. "Like war!"

"So what's stopping you?"

"We need your help."

Worm's mouth fell open as Rakesh explained. "You said something in the bus about the Civil War – only none of us know much about it..."

"You're actually asking me for advice?" Worm said in amazement.

"Well, sort of," admitted Jacko. "How long ago was it, then?"

"Stuart period, middle of the seventeenth century," Worm told them, doing some mental arithmetic. "Around three hundred and fifty years ago."

"That was about the last time Rakky scored before today, wasn't it?" Dazza joked.

"Didn't they chop the king's head off?" put in Ryan, racking his brain to be able to make some kind of relevant contribution to the discussion.

"Eventually," Worm replied. "King Charles's men, the Royalists, lost the war in the end to Cromwell's lot."

"Who were they?" asked Rakesh.

"The Roundheads, Parliament's troops. They were better organized."

"Right, I'll be this Cromwell guy, as

I'm captain," Jacko decided. "Who wants to be my Roundheads?"

"All those with short hair!" laughed Stopper.

It didn't quite work out like that, but finally the sixteen members of the squad were divided equally in number. It was agreed that anyone caught had to climb back down to the ground first before rejoining the battle.

"If this was a footie match, we'd thrash that lot easy!" laughed Ryan, flicking the ball up in the air on to his head.

"Well, it's not, and we need different tactics here," said Jacko as Worm quickly led his men up to higher ground. "Worm's already got the advantage of being above us. He's obviously taking it seriously."

Worm wasn't too surprised to find himself having to play King Charles – at Ryan's suggestion – but he rose to the part. "Right, come on, my brave Cavaliers. We've got to defend our territory against the riff-raff below."

"Long live the king!" cried Anil.

"OK, OK, don't get too carried away," said Worm. "You can be Prince Rupert, my nephew, and a daring cavalry commander."

"Fat lot of use that is without any horses," Anil replied.

Jacko, meanwhile, was circling his troops around the rear of the rock formation in pairs. "Keep out of sight as much as you can," he told them. "Yell for reinforcements if you need help."

"Let's try and capture the king," Ryan smirked. "Worm shouldn't be too difficult to ambush somewhere."

"Good idea. The war will be over if they lose their leader," said Jacko. "Dazza, Rakesh, you two follow us. Watch out for Worm."

Armed with a couple of snowballs

each, scooped out of rocky hollows, Jacko's Roundheads wound their way between the rocks, clambering up higher whenever the opportunity allowed. The Royalists were armed, too, and Dazza only just ducked in time to avoid a well-aimed missile.

"We've been spotted!" he hissed. "Keep your heads down."

Shouts from nearby confirmed other clashes between opposing forces and Stopper's voice was heard claiming the

capture of a prisoner. "Down you go, pal, have a good trip!" he chortled.

As snow began to fall again, however, the king still proved elusive. Worm and Anil were taking shelter from the weather and the enemy beneath a ledge of overhanging rock, but their temporary hide-out was soon discovered.

"There he is!" whooped Ryan. "We've got him now. Attack!"

A flurry of snowballs splattered against the ledge above them and while

the enemy were reloading, Worm and Anil bolted for freedom. "Through that gap down there!" Worm cried out, pointing the way. "Let's go, fast!"

"Don't let them escape!" ordered Jacko. "After them, men!"

The four Roundheads scrabbled across the slippery, white-coated rocks on to a narrow track leading to a low channel between two boulders. When they squirmed through to the other side, they were astonished to find Worm and Anil with their hands raised, as if in surrender.

"Nowhere else to run, eh?" laughed Dazza. "Dead end, is it?"

Their delight was short-lived. They found themselves staring down the long barrel of a gun – and the soldier pointing it at them might have stepped straight from the pages of a history book about the English Civil War...

5 Blizzard!

"How many are yer?" growled the soldier.

Worm turned slowly and looked into the frightened faces of his teammates. "Only six," he replied, desperately hoping that no more would squeeze through the gap.

"Dunno what you're all doin' here, dressed in yer fancy clothes," the soldier muttered, eyeing their coloured coats and jeans. "But y'can tell yer story t'my commandin' officer. Get movin'."

He motioned them down the snow-covered rocks with the barrel of his musket. Worm led the boys in single file down the winding track, Anil sandwiched between him and Jacko. Dazza and Rakesh followed close behind, with the soldier's gun prodding Ryan in the back to keep them all shuffling forwards on shaky legs through the thick snow.

Howling blasts of wind whipped the snow horizontally into their faces, cruelly cutting into their flesh, but there was no use in protesting. They knew that this was no game they were playing now. This was for real.

Worm shook his head. "It's happened again!" he murmured in disbelief. "Looks like we've somehow gone and slipped back in time to the Civil War itself. We've been captured by a Roundhead!"

The soldier was handicapped just as much by the blizzard conditions on the exposed rock above the moor. At one point they all had to stop, simply because they could not see through the stinging snow. They raised their arms to protect themselves and that was the moment when Ryan struck.

"Aaaghh!"

The soldier's scream caused them all to whirl round as he toppled off the track into a deep snowdrift several metres below. They stood transfixed, watching the man trying to claw himself back to his feet and flail around in the snow for his gun.

"Hit him smack in the face with the ball," cried Ryan, picking up the football where it lay in a mound of snow. "C'mon, leg it like mad."

They didn't argue, but running was impossible. Sheer panic, however, enabled them to pound down the last part of the track and into a clump of trees where they paused briefly to catch their breath.

"What happened back there?" demanded Jacko.

Ryan forced a grin. "The guy must have stumbled in the snow and lost his balance on that narrow bit – and I sort of helped him on his way!"

"You were taking an incredible risk," Dazza gasped.

"Didn't have time to think. I just smashed the ball at him and over he went. Best drop-kick I ever did!"

"What's going on?" wailed Anil. "I don't understand. Where are we?"

His friends looked at each other. Anil was the only one among them who hadn't shared their previous adventure. "Tell you later," said Rakesh. "When we've managed to work things out a bit more ourselves."

"Right now," Worm said decisively, "we've got to put some distance between us and that Roundhead. He's going to come after us, and this time he won't be asking questions."

"Shoot first, like me, you mean?" put in Ryan.

Worm nodded. "He was probably some kind of lookout man up there for the rest of his Parliamentary troop. They must be camped not far away."

"You reckon this is the actual Civil War, then, Worm?" said Dazza.

"I'm sure of it," he replied, and gave a grin. "Just as well he didn't know I was King Charles or we might really have been in big trouble!"

"Where are we going?" cried Anil as they set off at a slow jog.

"Another good question!" grunted Rakesh. "As far away as we can from that bloke with the gun, I hope."

"Won't he be able to follow our footsteps in the snow?"

Worm tried to reassure Anil, as well as himself, with his answer. "The weather's far worse here than it was back ... er ... you know, back where we came from. The snow's so heavy, it's covering our tracks pretty quickly by the look of it."

"There's tons of the stuff," Dazza panted. "I'm just about done in, slogging through it. I vote we find some shelter and lie low for a bit."

"Agreed!" said Jacko. "Let's make for that hill over there and see if we can hide somewhere out of this wind at least."

They trekked up the steep hill, fearful of being confronted again by angry soldiers. Jacko and Ryan went scouting ahead and soon doubled back to the main group. "There's a sort of small cave in the cliff further on," Jacko reported. "It's dry and pretty well hidden."

The boys reached it almost exhausted. They slumped down close together with their backs against the rock and tried to make some sense of their situation. They were talking in whispers, with Worm doing his best to make Anil understand why things had changed so much.

Rakesh had volunteered to stand guard for a while, keeping a lookout for signs of anybody approaching. "Ssshh!" he hissed urgently. "I think I heard some voices."

They hardly dared to breathe, flattening themselves to the rocky ground as the wind carried the sounds of men arguing. Worm looked down to their left and saw three soldiers – Roundheads, as far as he could tell – trudging through the snow along some kind of trail below where

they were all cowering.

The soldiers were clearly not best pleased with life, and Worm wondered whether one of them was in fact the sentry. He rested his head on his arm, praying for them to pass by, when there was a sudden, deafening noise in his ear. Worm jolted up and his heart lurched as he realized what it was – the jangling, electronic beeps of his watch!

The others turned agonized faces his way as Worm yanked off his gloves to try and cut out the tell-tale beeps. In his haste and the cold, he was all fingers and thumbs, and it seemed like an age before he succeeded.

He shot a terrified glance at the trail, expecting to see the soldiers charging towards them, and then let out a loud gasp of relief. The men were already out of sight, the whistling wind obviously drowning out any other sounds.

"Five o'clock," Worm said, sheepishly. "Time for tea!"

6 Get digging

The boys stayed in their hide-out a long time, not daring to move.

"Best to wait till dark," Jacko suggested. "Then we'll try and get back somehow to the rocks."

"You know which way to go?" queried Rakesh, but guessed the answer.

"We can always find some nice soldiers to ask directions," Ryan sighed.

The blanket of snow had made everywhere look much the same and visibility was still poor. Their flight had been too panicky for them to take much notice of any landmarks that might serve to guide their return.

The boys fell silent, huddled in their coats for any remaining warmth, but they were growing very cold. A few of them managed only a fitful doze, troubled by scary images of guns and blizzards.

"Why does this time-warp business keep happening to us?" muttered Ryan. "It doesn't make any sense."

"Must be a reason for it," Worm murmured in reply.

"You said that last time."

"Well, I was right, wasn't I? So maybe there's a reason again."

"Like what?"

"How should I know? I haven't got a crystal ball."

"I thought a crystal ball was for looking into the future, not the past," interrupted Rakesh.

"C'mon," Dazza urged everyone. "Let's risk it now. We're gonna freeze to death if we stay here much longer."

Grumbling, they got stiffly to their feet like a bunch of crotchety old men, pounding their arms to try and get some circulation going again.

"I'm hungry," moaned Anil.

"We all are," Jacko said. "But where are we going to get some food round here? We can't exactly nip round to the local supermarket!"

"That watch of yours isn't a compass as well, is it?" Rakesh wondered.

"No, only a time machine," Worm said, surprisingly wittily. "But I've been thinking."

"Oh, no!" Ryan groaned. "We're in enough of a mess as it is."

Worm ignored him. "I reckon this trail below must be an old packhorse route, you know, like the one going over the bridge at Oakbrooke. They were used to carry goods all over the country. It must lead somewhere."

"Are you saying we should follow it?" asked Jacko.

"I suppose so – but in the opposite direction to those soldiers."

As no one else could suggest any better idea, they pulled up their hoods and picked their way down from the shelter until they reached the narrow trail. It wasn't snowing quite as much as before, but every step was an effort through the knee-deep snow that had already fallen. Braced against the wind, heads down, they never even saw what awaited them further along the trail until they walked right into it.

"Halt! Who goes there? Speak or I shoot!"

For the second time in a few hours, the boys found themselves looking down the barrel of a musket. "Don't shoot!" Jacko croaked out. "We're only kids."

The man in front of them visibly relaxed, but he still kept the weapon

aimed in their direction. "Where have you come from?" he demanded.

That was not a question that could easily be answered. Worm made the only response he could think of – the truth. "We got caught out in the blizzard. We've been sheltering in a little cave back there."

"The hermit's cave?"

"I don't know its name."

As another man stepped forward, the boys became aware of a number of heavily-laden horses standing in the snow beyond. This second man was also armed, but neither of them had the look of soldiers. "You come from Barwell to meet us?" he asked, alarmed. "If you have, keep your distance. We don't want the plague off you."

"We haven't got the plague," Rakesh piped up. "We only came here to play football."

Ryan held up the ball as proof, but the

man didn't seem to understand. "You sure you ain't got the plague?"

"Positive," Worm stated firmly. "Are you trying to get to Barwell?"

"Aye, that we are," said the first man, lowering his musket. "I'm the jagger, in charge of this 'ere packhorse train, and this food's got to get through to them brave people. Up to Ned and me to see they don't starve."

"Bet they gone and given up on us in this weather," Ned said miserably. "Keep getting stuck in drifts. Should've been there hours ago."

"Might've made it, too, if we hadn't been attacked by them Roundheads earlier," added the jagger. "Dirty thieves!"

"What happened?" asked Dazza, open-mouthed.

"Patrol took us by surprise, scared three other men off and stole five of our horses," Ned explained. "Soldiers ain't got no food of their own, so they go round robbing from honest folk."

"What, even supplies meant for Barwell?" Worm gasped.

"Aye," the jagger nodded. "Barwell's for the Royalists, see, since the start of this terrible war, so them Roundheads don't care."

"King's soldiers are just as bad," grunted Ned. "They'd steal our food as well, if they got a chance."

The jagger grew suspicious again. "Whose side you on, anyway?"

Worm tried to play it safe. "Nobody's," he answered. "We just want the war to end."

"Ain't no one not fed up with all this fighting," Ned said. "Ain't no sense to it. Set village against village, brother against brother."

"We can help you reach Barwell, if you like," Worm offered suddenly. "Seeing as there's only two of you now."

Ryan dragged him away by the arm. "Are you crazy, Worm? Why don't you learn to mind your own business?"

"It was you who wanted a reason for being here, and I reckon this is it," Worm snapped. "We need to see that all this stuff gets safely through to Barwell so the villagers don't starve to death. Got to make sure history comes true. We know that some people did survive the plague."

"Yeah, but will *we* live to tell the tale?"

Worm shrugged. "Only if we ever manage to get back to the future," he reasoned. "And this might be our route – along the old packhorse trail."

"Worth a shot," agreed Jacko, listening in. "At least it's better being with two armed men, if we happen to run into any more soldiers."

"Right, that's decided, then," Worm said with satisfaction and turned back to the jagger. "What do you want us to do?"

The man bent down, picked up a shovel and tossed it over to him. "Get digging," he grinned, showing his toothless gums. "And keep digging!"

The boys all grabbed shovels and began to dig feverishly with the men. One by one, the trapped horses were slowly freed from the drifts and helped to stagger out with their loaded panniers back on to more secure ground.

"Well, Prince Rupert," Worm panted, leaning wearily on his shovel for a minute. "Here are the horses you wanted for your cavalry!"

"No good, I'm too heavy for them now," Anil wheezed. "My wellies are full of snow!"

Once they were ready to move on again, the jagger stared at the strange group of young travellers. "Got many miles to cover yet, y'know," he told them. "Up steep hills and across the moors through all this snow into plague country. Then there's them hungry soldiers on the loose..."

He trailed off to let them form their own picture of the difficulties and dangers that lay ahead. "You young folk still willing to come with us to Barwell?"

The boys looked around at each other and nodded. "Put like that, we can't think of anywhere else better to go!" grinned Ryan, packing the football into the nearest pannier. "Lead on, Mr Jagger!"

7 Ambush!

"I don't think I'll ever want to see any snow again after this," gasped Dazza as they slogged up another long hill.

The packhorse trail took a zigzag course upwards, but in the deep snow, it was still very hard work on the leg muscles. The fitness of the young footballers was tested to the full, their fatigue made worse by the fear of raids.

Daylight had now gone, but mercifully the snowfall had eased and the reflection of the moonlight on the snow underfoot allowed them to pick their way forward. Every so often one of the animals would sink into a drift and need to be dug out before the train could continue.

Progress was slow, but they pressed on relentlessly. They were all driven by the knowledge that the lives of the survivors in Barwell depended on these supplies of food, clothing, blankets and fuel.

"At least this weather has kept most of them soldiers in their camps," grunted the jagger. "Usually this area is crawling with 'em."

Worm glanced nervously around him for the umpteenth time. "Think we've seen the last of them tonight, Mr Jagger?"

"Aye, reckon so, lad. Mind you, they're so hungry and miserable, some of 'em will risk anything to get a bite to eat."

Three cold, wet soldiers lay in ambush behind some boulders next to the pack-horse trail.

"Won't be long now afore they're here," said one. "This is a better spot to hit 'em than where we first saw 'em a while back."

"Easy pickings!" grinned a second. "Only got two guards. We'll put a bullet in the jagger and t'other will take flight."

"Let him go," said their leader. "It's the food we want – and some dry clothing."

He kept watch on top of the boulder until the packhorse train came into sight in the moonlight, struggling up the hill. The leader stared, unable to believe the evidence of his own eyes, and he jumped back down to his men on the ground.

"Change of plan," he hissed and then uttered a foul curse. "They must have got reinforcements from somewhere. I can see six men at least with the horses, maybe more."

"What we going to do, sir? Rather be hungry than dead."

"Can't attack them head on now,

we're outnumbered," the leader decided. "We'll let most of the train pass by and then strike at the tail. Should be able to make off with a few horses before the men at the front realize what's happening. Get ready and wait for my signal."

The Roundheads crouched behind the large boulders as the train laboured past. Worm, Anil and the jagger were leading the front horses, Dazza and Rakesh trudged along in the middle, with Jacko, Ryan and Ned bringing up the rear.

Suddenly the three soldiers stepped out into view, startling the horses near the back. One of them was about to fire his pistol, but then checked himself. "Cousin Ned! It's you!" he exclaimed.

"What's the matter?" snapped the leader. "Shoot him!"

"He's my cousin, sir."

"Shoot him, man!" came the command, but the hesitation proved crucial, giving Jacko and Ryan time to dive for cover among the rocks by the trail.

Ned was able to take action too. He raised his own musket and aimed at one of the Roundheads charging towards him, hitting him in the leg and sending him tumbling with a scream into the snow.

Then the boys heard another sharp crack and looked out to see Ned grasping his arm in pain, wounded by his cousin's delayed shot.

"C'mon, we've got to do something," cried Jacko when they saw two soldiers frantically cutting the ropes linking the last four horses with the rest of the train. "Grab some rocks, anything!"

It had all happened so quickly, yet to the terrified boys the whole incident took place in front of them as if they were watching a slow-motion replay. Their wide eyes recorded every little detail of the drama, and as they scrabbled for loose pieces of rock as weapons, they

also became aware of the arrival of
Dazza and Rakesh.

Dazza managed to snatch back one of
the stray horses and the soldiers
panicked, knowing their ambush had
been badly bungled. They were trapped.
Rocks rained at their heads and the leader fired his pistol blindly towards his
tormentors, the bullet splintering the
boulder above Ryan's head.

"Quick, let's get out of here!" yelled

the leader, and then he swore loudly as Rakesh struck him on the shoulder with a large lump of coal from one of the panniers. The Roundhead steadied himself and took careful aim at Jacko as he tried to help the handicapped Ned reload his musket.

"Watch out, sir!" cried Ned's cousin. Dazza had set the packhorse stampeding towards the soldiers with a hearty slap on its haunches and the leader never even saw it coming. The warning shout came too late for him to react.

As he was about to pull the trigger, the horse caught him a glancing blow with the wide pannier of coal on its back. The pistol flew up into the air and the Roundhead was sent spinning away into a snowdrift. Only Ryan realized how close Jacko had come to stopping a bullet.

The soldiers had had enough. Showered by further missiles of rock and coal, Ned's cousin helped the groggy leader to his feet. Together, they lifted up their wounded comrade, slung him across the panniers of the nearest horse and made their desperate escape back down the trail.

The jagger, with Worm and Anil, appeared on the scene at that moment and he fired a bullet over the soldiers' heads to see them off.

"Ha! They won't bother us again," he

laughed. "Well fought, my friends. How goes it with you, Ned?"

His partner managed a rueful smile. "My arm's sore, but just a flesh wound, I think. I'll be all right to carry on."

"We lost one of the horses, though," said Dazza. "Sorry."

"Don't fret, lad. Can't be helped," the jagger replied. "By the sound of it, we'd have lost the whole lot – and, aye, mebbe our lives as well – if you people hadn't been here."

"That man was your cousin," Jacko gasped. "I heard him say so and yet he still shot at you."

"That's what this war has done to families," Ned sighed. "I'd have shot him, too, given half a chance! We're on different sides now."

"Reckon Dazza saved Jacko's life there," Ryan told them all. "That Roundhead might have killed him, if the horse hadn't mown him down first."

"Thanks, Dazza," Jacko nodded, white-faced with shock now that the danger was over. "I owe you one."

"Best save I'll ever make," the goal-keeper grinned.

8 There and back again

The packhorse train continued its trek in the darkness across the windswept moors and it was late at night when the jagger called a halt.

"What have we stopped for now?" groaned Ryan. "Are we stuck again?"

"No, we're here!" cried Worm. "The jagger says Barwell's just through this wood on our left."

Rakesh was suddenly afraid. "We're not actually going right into the village, are we? I mean, this plague is for real."

Worm smiled. "Relax. This is as near

as we get. We've reached the wayside cross where the villagers do their trading with the outside world while they're in quarantine."

The tall stone cross loomed up into the night sky, silhouetted against the white landscape. "It's a well-known landmark round here," said Worm. "This is journey's end."

"Apart from having to turn round and go back again," Dazza grumbled.

"At least it'll be mostly downhill the other way," Jacko consoled him. "And you never know, we might even be able to hitch a ride once the horses have got rid of their loads."

The thought of having a lift back spurred them on as they started to empty the panniers. With Ned nursing his injured arm in a roughly-made sling, most of the work of clearing snow from around the cross and stacking all the provisions there fell upon the boys. They were so busy, they failed to realize at first that they were being watched.

Their arrival had attracted a crowd, even at this late hour. It seemed that the whole village, or at least what was left of its people, had ventured out into the cold night to welcome the packhorse train.

The men, women and children were stretched out in a line near the edge of the wood. They stayed at a safe distance from the traders, straining to see what had been brought. Many knew Ned and the jagger well from previous visits and shouted their greetings across the gap between them.

"You're a sight for sore eyes – and empty bellies!"

"Our thanks and our prayers for risking your lives to reach us."

"Didn't think you'd ever make it here."

Ned pointed towards the boys unloading the supplies. "Neither did we!

And we wouldn't have done if *they* hadn't turned up out of the blue."

"Aye, that's right," the jagger confirmed. "They even fought off some Roundheads for us."

"God bless them!" cried one of the women and the time travellers found themselves showered with praise.

Then it was down to business, with many questions to be answered.

"What's in them sacks over there?"

"Did you bring all that cloth we ordered?"

"What's the price of the salt?"

The negotiations had to be based upon trust. Due to the danger of passing on the disease, the villagers weren't able to inspect what they were buying in advance and the sellers couldn't count their cash.

After much haggling over the value of the goods, agreement was finally reached

and the money was placed in a trough of vinegar to disinfect the coins. As the villagers began to carry away the sacks and boxes, the footballers noticed some youngsters hanging back in the trees' shadows.

"Good job it's stopped snowing, they're just in rags," observed Jacko. "Look how skinny they are, too!"

"Now I've seen them, I'll never again say I'm starving," said Dazza.

"One of them is probably Will Buxton, Daniel's ancestor," said Worm. "The kid I told you about who did the soccer picture on the church wall."

"Well, let's find out," Ryan decided and called out across the wide space that divided them. "Will? Will Buxton. Are you there?"

For a time no one moved, then a small boy, almost buried under a large cap, was shoved forward by several of the others. "This is Will Buxton," came the nervous reply. "What's he done?"

"Nothing. It's all right, Will, we just want to give you a message from a distant relative," Ryan yelled over to him. "He says don't worry, everything's gonna work out fine! Now watch this..."

Ryan picked up the football and demonstrated a little game of keep-it-up, juggling the ball on his feet, knees and head. It wasn't too skilful in his wellies, and he lost control several times, but he drew a very curious audience ever closer to get a better view.

Jacko joined in, playing a spot of head tennis with Ryan, with Dazza sometimes leaping between them to grab the ball in his hands.

"Good game, eh, Will?" shouted Ryan. "Want to play?"

"Hey, just a minute!" cried Rakesh. "You can't invite them over here. The ball isn't all we might catch off them."

"Don't be stupid. I'm not trying to set up a return match with Barwell," Ryan scoffed. "Just booting the ball to each other across the gap won't do any harm, will it?"

Ryan didn't give anyone a chance to object. He lofted the ball towards the village boys who scrabbled in the snow for it like a rugby scrum. It was little Will who emerged out of the ruck triumphant, holding the ball above his mop of fair hair in delight. He'd lost his cap in the free-for-all and Worm gasped as he saw how much Will looked like Daniel.

Will tried to drop-kick the ball back, but missed it completely and lost his balance. He toppled over into the snow to great shrieks of laughter from the other children.

Somebody else ran up to kick the ball but it didn't go very far. It sat teed-up on a heap of snow in no-man's-land between the two groups, as if daring

someone to make the first move. Despite their excitement, the young villagers knew that they must not make any contact with outsiders.

It was Worm who walked forward. "I'll get it," he said calmly. "Then that's the end of the game for us – but just the start of it for them."

All eyes were on Worm as he stopped by the ball. "We want you to have this football to play with," he told the children. "You keep it."

With that, he gave the football the hardest kick he could manage in his wellies, sending it whirling away over their heads towards the trees. They all turned, laughing and screaming, to run after the ball.

All except one. Will Buxton still stood facing Worm, no more than twenty metres from him, but worlds apart. "Thank you," he said shyly, then shot Worm the cheekiest of grins and raced off after his pals.

"Well, there goes another ball," Ryan sighed. "Dad will have to go and buy a new one now, we're running out of them."

"Don't think he'd want that one back, if he ever knew where it'd been," remarked Rakesh. "Let's just hope they make good use of it."

"Oh, they will, you can be sure of that," Worm smiled.

Perched astride a lurching packhorse, their feet inside the empty panniers, may not have been the most comfortable ride in the world, but the exhausted boys preferred it to walking.

The return journey did not seem to take half as long, even though they had to keep dismounting to lead the horses past obstacles or around snowdrifts. At least that gave some relief to their sore bottoms.

Of the soldiers, there was thankfully no further sign. "Don't reckon they'll be interested in us much now," said the jagger, trying to reassure his companions. "They know we've got no food left."

Suddenly, Dazza let out a loud whoop. "Over on the right, look! Those must be our rocks again. I recognize their shape. We're back!"

Anil peered around as if expecting to see all the tents and caravans, and Worm saw his disappointment. "Not yet, I'm afraid, Anil. We're still three centuries too early!"

"No good hanging about waiting to put the clocks forward, then," Jacko quipped. "C'mon, the only way is up."

The boys jumped down off the pack-horses to say their farewells to the traders. "Thanks for guiding us safely back," said Worm.

" 'Tis us – and the people of Barwell –

who must thank *you*," the jagger replied. "Without all your help, we'd never have got through to 'em."

"You sure you want to be left here?" asked Ned doubtfully. "You're in the middle of nowhere. How long will it take you to get back home?"

"That depends," Worm shrugged. "Might well take some time!"

The boys began to scramble along the snow-laden track up the side of the rocky outcrop. "Just hope that sentry isn't still around," puffed Anil. "Thought I was seeing things when you and me went through that gap."

"You get used to it," Worm said. "This is proving a real weird week."

The six boys stood in front of the narrow channel between two large boulders, looking at one another. "What happens if we're still stuck in Stuart times on the other side?" murmured Rakesh, voicing their fears.

"Guess we could always get a job working for old Jagger!" said Dazza.

"Either that or join up with Cromwell's lot," muttered Ryan. "At least we'd know we're on the winning side."

"Right, who's going first?" said Jacko, glancing at Worm.

"I think you've just been volunteered," Rakesh whispered to him.

"OK, better than standing here for ever," he said, forcing a smile. "See you all later – I hope – in about three hundred and fifty years!"

Worm bent down and disappeared through the channel. The others waited and called to him, but there was no response. "He's either made it or fallen off the edge of the rock," said Ryan. "C'mon, let's go after him."

As the group emerged, they were almost blinded by the daylight reflecting off the smooth covering of snow on the rocks.

"Great stuff, Jacko, you've captured the king!" yelled Stopper.

Stopper was about to grab hold of Worm when he looked at all his friends more closely. They were staring back at him in disbelief.

"What's happened to you lot?" he gasped. "Oh, no! Not again, surely!"

The boys gazed down at their filthy coats and then grinned at each other. "We've done it!" cried Dazza. "We've actually made it back in one piece."

"Well, more or less," added Anil, examining the tears in the knees of his jeans.

"You went and left me behind this time," Stopper accused them.

"Sorry, we didn't have a chance to send any invitations," Ryan grinned. "That'll teach you to mark up more tightly. You let us get too far away from you."

"How far away?" he asked enviously.

"A long, long way," groaned Rakesh. "My feet are killing me, not to mention my backside. We must have covered a million miles!"

"Don't talk stupid," said Stopper crossly. "I saw you all go through there just a minute ago. I bombed up here to follow you."

Worm smiled broadly. "You mean nobody's missed us?"

"'Course not. It's not even teatime yet."

"Have to adjust my watch," Worm said. "I'm still on Civil War time."

Jacko breathed a sigh of relief. "At least that's saved us having to come up with some ridiculous story to explain where we've been all night!"

Speedie appeared on a rock above them. "Is the war over now?"

"It is for us," answered Dazza. "Though I think the real thing's probably got some way to go yet!"

Speedie didn't understand. "Anybody want a game of footie instead?" he asked. "Where's the ball?"

"Bet that's exactly what Dad's gonna say, too!" muttered Ryan.

"I think some other kids have gone off with it," Anil told him.

"What about a snowball fight, then?" Speedie persisted. "Snow's starting to get heavier."

"Sorry," said Jacko, shaking his head. "We're going back down to the tents for a rest. Reckon we've all had enough of this white stuff for one day, thanks."

"*Any* day!" stressed Rakesh. "Past, present or future..."

TIME RANGERS

The time tour continues with Time Rangers 3.
A Race Against Time

Captain Tony opened the scoring immediately with an expertly judged, double-handed catch off the ceiling. Dazza was left gaping and flat-footed as the ball was gleefully hurled past him into the net.

"OK, so maybe they play the game a bit different here," he shrugged, a sickly grin trying to hide his embarrassment.

Goalscoring, future-style, was not exactly a rarity. Goals flew in at both ends almost as often as they do in basketball, mainly because the players were also allowed to handle the ball. Catching and throwing were just as common as kicking.

By the time the Rangers players began to adjust to the new rules, the game had reached the quarter-stage break and they were losing heavily.

"Twelve–five!" snorted Dazza in disgust. "Ridiculous. I don't stand a chance when the shooter can just chuck the ball in with his hands."